This Book Belongs to:

_____

For Nana Kitty

Maisie Mae's
Christmas Cheer

By Stephanie Jane Markham · Pictures by Graziella Miligi

Copyright © 2021 Stephanie Jane Markham ISBN: 978-0-578-33603-9

First Printing, 2021

It's two weeks till Christmas
and I cannot wait!
Caroling, candy canes,
staying up late.

Christmas is snowfall,
a visit from Gran.

Rosey-cheeked babies
pushed in a pram.

Candied pears
and pfeffernusse.

School bells ring
and kids let loose!

The snow comes down softly.
There's a fireplace to light.
We'll snuggle together
as the tree twinkles bright.

Mom makes cocoa and
marshmallows too.
We talk about fun things
we're going to do.

When we go sledding,
I'll bundle up warm.
Hat, scarf, and mittens
in case there's a storm.

We'll build a snow village.
An igloo for me!

Then visit our good friends,
the Snow family.

Mom, Dad and Jack
Snowman are so very nice.
They'll serve us pink
donuts and lemonade ice.

Letty and Duncan dance in the snow. Simon and Sabrina put on a show!

Simon plays trumpet.
Sabrina, she sings.

Then, I'll learn to skate
with both of the twins.

Emma's fantastic.
She leaps and she spins!

My legs are so shaky,
I'm afraid I will fall.
But when I don't try things
it's no fun at all.
Emma says, "Go ahead, Maisie!
Give it a go."
She holds onto my hand
and doesn't let go.

"I'm skating!" I say
and I skate some more.
Fun with friends
is what Christmas is for.
The best presents to give
aren't wrapped with a bow.
You take Christmas cheer
wherever you go.

Christmas reminds me
of all that I've got.
And helps me remember
those that do not.

The Christmas spirit can last
all the year round.
Just open your heart,
cause that's where it's found.

It's love and some kindness
and a whole lot of cheer
that makes Christmas time
the best time of year.

Merry Christmas!
Happy Kwanza!
Happy Hanukkah too!
From the Sunnyside Kids
and your friend, Letty Lou.

Made in the USA
Las Vegas, NV
12 December 2021

37232864R00021